# RICOCHET

## THE REACHER EXPERIMENT BOOK 8

Jude Hardin

# 1

You don't need a map of Louisville to find Rock Wahlman's house. Just follow the signs to Churchill Downs, take a left on Fifth, and look for the bungalow with the closed-in porch and the portable steel yard sign.

*Wahlman Investigative Services.*

The sign is nothing special.

The porch has a story.

A few years before Wahlman was born, a middle-aged couple with a couple of teenagers still in the house got talked into some new siding and an additional two hundred square feet of living space. Probably some sort of E-Z payment plan. Probably not as E-Z as the salesperson made it sound. The construction crew did a fine job, but the architectural design is never going to win any awards for curb appeal. The front façade looks like a giant shoebox with a door and a window cut into it. Like something drawn with crayons.

Soon after the project was finished, one of the teenagers won some sort of contest and got to meet a popular singer of the day, a guy named Jessie Reddington, one of those iconic megastars who still got radio play on certain stations forty-some years later. The teenager met Reddington right there in the renovated space that used to be the front porch. Right there in Wahlman's office. Or so the story went. The neighbor who had told Wahlman about it tended to exaggerate.

Wahlman stood there on the front stoop and waved goodbye to his stepdaughter as she backed out of the driveway, off to attend an orientation session at one of the freshman dormitories at the University of Louisville. Kasey stood there beside him, brushing tears away with the back of her hand.

"It's just a couple of miles down the road," Wahlman said.

"I know, but it's still sad. Don't you think it's sad?"

"What's so sad about it?"

"My baby's all grown up."

Rock Wahlman and Kasey Stielson had gotten married on New Year's Eve, 2099.

The dawn of a brand new century.

The dawn of a brand new life.

In a few months, they would celebrate their second anniversary. There would be parties and fireworks and all kinds of revelry all over the world, and it would be that way on every anniversary for as long as they lived. They planned to rent a hotel room with a view of the river and turn out the lights and open the drapes and pretend it was all just for them.

Kasey had chosen to settle in Louisville because of its

proximity to Nashville, where her parents lived. It was close enough, but not *too* close, she'd said. Wahlman wasn't particular about where they stayed, as long as they were together, and as long as there was a big enough population for him to make a living.

"I have a client coming by in a little while," he said.

"You have a client? Really?"

"Don't act like it's such an unusual event."

"You have to admit, it's been pretty slow lately," Kasey said.

"It'll get better."

"You keep saying that."

"It will."

There was a sycamore tree in the front yard. Some kind of bird was up in the branches, near the top, chirping nervously, hidden from sight by the fat leaves.

"I'm going out again today," Kasey said. "I have several more interviews. In fact, I better get going. The first one's at nine."

"It's not like we're broke," Wahlman said.

"I know. But I want to work. I need something to do."

"Okay."

"Who's your client?"

"I'll tell you about it at dinner tonight," Wahlman said. "And you can tell me about your interviews."

"And Natalie can tell us all about her orientation," Kasey said. "And maybe I can finally talk her into staying here and commuting."

Wahlman doubted it, but he didn't say anything. He turned and opened the door and followed Kasey into the house.

# 2

The client was late.

Anxiously awaiting her arrival, Wahlman had been pacing from one end of his office to the other for thirty minutes or so. The fluffy ginger tabby they called Alice had marched alongside him for a while, but had grown weary of it and had curled up to take a nap on the bookshelf in the corner. Alice had shown up on the stoop one day back in June, and Natalie had let her inside and had fed her, and that was that. Now Alice was part of the family.

And like the rest of the family, she liked to eat on a regular basis.

Kasey was right. It had been slow lately. Wahlman had been thinking about getting some kind of side job, just to make ends meet. A job delivering pizzas or something. Kasey's parents were wealthy. They were millionaires. But Wahlman refused to ask them for help, unless it was an emergency. He'd decided that he would make it as a private investigator, or that he would do something else. Lately it had been looking more and more like something else.

He looked at his watch, sat at his desk, grabbed a pencil from the ceramic teapot he used for a caddy and started drumming on the mousepad. He did that for a couple of minutes, and then he slid the pencil back into the teapot and got up and peeked through the blinds and saw one of the most famous movie stars on the planet climb out of a rusty old hatchback and step onto the sidewalk.

At twenty-nine, Janelle Pierce had already been nominated for seven Academy Awards and three Golden Globes. She hadn't actually won any awards yet, but most of the critics seemed to think it was just a matter of time. She'd made an effort to disguise herself, but Wahlman knew it was her. The junk car and the bandana and the dark glasses weren't quite enough. They didn't cover that neck, and that chin, and those lips.

Janelle had grown up across the river, in Jeffersonville, and still visited the area frequently. Wahlman opened the door before she had a chance to knock.

"Are you Rock Wahlman?" she said.

"Yes. Come on in."

Wahlman held the door while she stepped across the threshold. She pulled the glasses off first, and then the scarf. Her hair was lighter than it had been in her last movie. Her eyes were the color of the sky in April.

"Is that a church pew?" she said.

"Yes. Please, have a seat."

The pew had been there when Wahlman bought the place. Seven feet long, solid oak. Wahlman figured it had a story too, but he hadn't heard it yet. His client set her things

5

down and nestled in by the armrest closest to the door.

"I should probably go ahead and make it clear that I'm not her," she said.

"Pardon me?" Wahlman said.

"I'm not her."

"But on the phone you said—"

"I know what I said. And I know it's not the right thing to do. But it makes life easier sometimes. Appointments. Tables at restaurants. Whatever."

The resemblance was remarkable. Wahlman didn't bother telling her that there had been no need for the deception, that his calendar was as open as a bourbon bottle on Derby Day.

"So who are you?" he said, reaching for a pencil and a notebook.

"Rokki Rhodes," she said.

"Like the ice cream?"

She spelled it. Wahlman wrote it down.

"What can I do for you, Ms. Rhodes?"

"You can call me Rokki."

"Okay. Why did you decide to—"

"Someone's following me," she said.

"Someone's following you?"

"Stalking. I guess that's the word. I dance in a club. Some guy's been coming to every show, sitting in front, staring at me the whole time."

Wahlman drummed the pencil on the mousepad.

"Isn't that what guys do in those kinds of places?" he said.

"He's creeping me out."

"Has he tried to talk to you? Has he approached you outside of the club?"

"No. He just sits there and stares."

"Has he called or sent texts to your phone? Has he harassed you on social media? Anything like that?"

"No."

"It doesn't sound like he's breaking any laws."

"I know. That's why I came to you instead of the police."

"What exactly is it that you want me to do?" Wahlman said.

"Tell him to stop."

"And if he doesn't?"

"I want this guy out of my life. I want you to do whatever it takes."

Wahlman drummed the pencil on the mousepad some more.

"Are you suggesting what I think you're suggesting?" he said.

"Whatever it takes," Rokki said.

"You want me to beat him up? Break some bones, maybe?"

"Whatever it takes."

"Sorry. I don't think I can help you."

Rokki shifted in her seat.

"Why not?" she said.

"That's just not the kind of thing I do," Wahlman said.

He'd jumped through a lot of hoops to get his P.I. license. He'd driven down to New Orleans back in the summer of 2098 and had turned himself in on a variety of charges, including two counts of first-degree murder. He'd spent a day and a half in the detention center before posting bail, and he'd spent six months fighting the charges, represented by a struggling young attorney who took the case pro bono because of the publicity it was sure to generate. Once he'd been cleared of any wrongdoing, there was still a matter of having the records expunged before the state of Kentucky—or any other state in the Union—would accept an application for professional licensure. He'd jumped through a lot of hoops, and he wasn't about to put his career in jeopardy by taking a job that involved intimidation—and maybe even physical violence—no matter how much he needed the money.

"Sorry I wasted your time," Rokki said.

"Me too," Wahlman said.

Rokki stood and put the sunglasses back on.

"I'm working tonight," she said. "Laupin's. Stop by if you change your mind."

She exited the office. Wahlman stood and peeked through the blinds, saw her climb into the rusty old hatchback and drive away.

Alice was still snoozing on the bookshelf.

Wahlman walked back to his desk and opened a browser and wrote down some phone numbers of some of the pizza places in the area.

The ones that delivered.

# 3

Wahlman followed Kasey into the kitchen. She was carrying a large brown paper bag. One side of the bag was darkened with something that had spilled out a little.

"Chinese again?" Wahlman said.

"Yeah. Sorry. I have too much going on to think about cooking anything tonight."

"Too much going on?"

"I got a job," Kasey said, lifting one of the greasy food cartons out of the greasy paper bag.

"What kind of job?" Wahlman said.

"I'm going to be driving a route for a vending machine company. Collecting money from the machines, maybe doing some light maintenance sometimes. I have to go to Lexington for two days of training. I have to be there at eight o'clock in the morning, so—"

"You're going to be working in Lexington?"

"No. Here in Louisville. But the training's in Lexington."

"Oh."

"Where's Natalie?" Kasey said.

"She called a while ago," Wahlman said. "She's staying at the dorm tonight."

Kasey stopped pulling cartons out of the bag.

"What?" she said. "Already? She hasn't even taken any of her things over there yet."

"She has a change of clothes with her. She said she'll start moving her stuff tomorrow."

"Classes don't start until next week. Why would she want to—"

"She said something about a rush party at one of the sorority houses."

"And you told her that was okay?"

"She didn't really ask for permission," Wahlman said. "She just called to let us know that she wouldn't be home tonight."

"I don't like the idea of her going to some wild party," Kasey said. "And that only leaves us with one car. The only reason I agreed to let her stay in the dorm in the first place was so we wouldn't—"

"When she comes home tomorrow, I'll help her move, and then I'll keep the car," Wahlman said. "It's not that big of a deal. I don't need to go anywhere in the morning anyway."

"I thought you had a client."

"Not anymore."

"What happened?"

Wahlman explained what had happened.

"You don't have to go to work for that vending machine company," he said. "I'm going to start looking around for a side job."

"What kind of side job?"

"Delivering pizzas or something."

Kasey sighed.

"That would suck," she said.

"So would not being able to make the mortgage payment," Wahlman said.

"It's not like we're going to be out on the street or anything. Every time I talk to Daddy, he makes it clear that—"

"You know how I feel about taking money from your parents," Wahlman said.

"Yeah. I know. Anyway, I'm going to go ahead and take the job I was offered today. Which means that I'm going to have to get up and leave the house very early tomorrow morning."

"How early?"

"At least by six. I'll be staying at a hotel in Lexington tomorrow night. I'll call you and let you know which one. And don't worry. The company's paying for everything."

Wahlman thought about trying to talk her out of taking the job, but he didn't. Once Kasey had her mind set on doing something, she did it, no matter what. It would have been like trying to talk a train off its track.

Wahlman opened a cabinet and pulled out some plates.

"Let's eat," he said. "Before it gets cold."

# 4

Kasey was long gone by the time Wahlman climbed out of bed the next morning. He looked out the window and saw that the driveway was empty, remembered that Natalie still had the car he usually drove. He figured he would call her in an hour or so, try to get her things moved over to the dorm fairly early, try to get out and put in some applications for employment. Better in person than online, he thought. Especially at places like pizza joints.

Wahlman switched on the television on the way to the kitchen. The news was on. The weather forecast. Sunny and hot, with a chance of afternoon thundershowers. Wahlman wondered what kind of credentials you needed to be a weatherperson. He figured he could guess as well as the people working at the local news channels. Maybe that could be his new career. *And now, Rock Wahlman with the weather.* It had a nice ring to it, he thought. He was dipping a measuring scoop into a can of coffee when the weather report was cut short. Some sort of breaking story. Something about a hiker finding the body of a celebrity lookalike up in

Iroquois Park, up in the woods, near one of the horseshoe-shaped viewing areas known among locals as the lookouts.

Wahlman's jaw dropped. He stepped into the living room and turned the volume up on the television. The lookalike had been stabbed. Multiple times. Dozens of shallow wounds. The hiker who'd found her had thought she was actually Janelle Pierce. The reporter covering the story seemed to be disappointed that she wasn't. He never actually said the words *just a stripper*, but that was the vibe you got. He made sure to mention how slow and painful her death had probably been, just in case anyone listening hadn't figured that out.

Wahlman slumped into the armchair in the corner, immediately started wondering if he could have prevented the tragedy. Rokki Rhodes had come to him for help, and he'd told her no.

And now she was dead.

Of course none of it was actually Wahlman's fault. He knew that. But he'd been a Master–At-Arms in the United States Navy for twenty years. The law enforcement officer inside of him just couldn't stand back and watch from the sidelines.

He needed his car. He tried to call Natalie. No answer. He left a message, went back to the kitchen, glanced over to make sure there was plenty of food in Alice's food dish and plenty of water in her water bowl, padded to the bedroom and put some clothes on and headed outside. He walked to the corner and took a left at the same stop sign Rokki had taken a left at yesterday, made his way up to the car lot.

Charlie Freckman's Used Cars. Wahlman helped Charlie with security sometimes. In exchange, Charlie allowed him to take extended test drives sometimes.

Wahlman knew exactly where to find Charlie at that time of the morning. He was in the office, sitting behind a heavily-scarred wooden desk, punching numbers into an electric adding machine, a relic that had originally belonged to his great grandfather.

Charlie smiled when Wahlman walked into the room. His teeth and the plastic housing on the adding machine were approximately the same shade of yellow. From years of tobacco abuse. Probably multiple generations of it, in the case of the adding machine.

"How's it going, Rock?" Charlie said.

"I need a car," Wahlman said.

"Is it going to smell like cat piss when you bring it back?"

"I'll buy you a can of air freshener," Wahlman said. "I'll buy you two. One for the car, and one for your breath."

Charlie laughed, opened the desk drawer and pulled out a familiar set of keys.

"It's parked around back," he said.

"You're going to make me drive that thing again?"

"It's a classic."

"It's a piece of shit."

Charlie laughed some more.

"Greg's going to need the night off tonight," he said. "Think you could watch the place for me?"

"Think you could give me a better vehicle?" Wahlman said.

Charlie lit a cigarette, took a long drag, exhaled toward the ceiling.

"Which one do you want?" he said.

"I want the black one parked out front."

"You're joking, right?"

"You asked which one I wanted."

"Yeah, but—"

"Don't worry. I'm not taking Alice to the vet today."

"Why do you need a car? You have a client?"

"Kind of."

"What's that mean?" Charlie said.

"I'll tell you later," Wahlman said. "Can I have the car or not?"

"Why do you need such a fast one?"

"Because you never know," Wahlman said.

Charlie opened the desk drawer and pulled out another set of keys.

"I need it back on the lot by the time I leave at seven this evening," he said.

"Okay."

"And I need you to watch the place for me tonight."

Wahlman nodded. He grabbed the keys and exited the office, walked to the front of the lot and slid into the driver seat of an automobile that was probably worth more than his house. He started the engine, sat there and tried to remember if his insurance bill had been paid, decided that it had, shifted the transmission into gear and headed downtown.

# 5

Wahlman entered the police station, walked to the front desk and identified himself as a licensed private investigator with a possible lead on a homicide. The officer behind the counter didn't seem impressed. She told him to have a seat. And it wasn't even a very comfortable seat. And Wahlman doubted that the other dozen or so men and women sitting there were licensed private investigators. He doubted that some of them were even licensed drivers.

He waited.

An hour or so and two terrible vending machine cups of coffee later, a man in a suit stepped up to the waiting area and called his name.

"I'm Detective Brannelly," the man said. "Follow me."

Wahlman followed him to a door marked POLICE ONLY, and then into a room with a bunch of cubicles and a tile floor that was way past due for stripping and waxing. Brannelly stepped into one of the cubicles and sat behind a small steel desk and motioned for Wahlman to sit in the chair in front of it.

"I'm here regarding the Rokki Rhodes case," Wahlman said.

"Who?" Brannelly said.

"Rokki Rhodes. It was on the news this morning."

Brannelly clicked some keys on his computer keyboard.

"Here it is," he said. "What about it?"

"I'm a private investigator," Wahlman said, pulling his wallet out and flipping it open to display his license. "Ms. Rhodes came to my office yesterday, claimed some guy was stalking her at the club where she worked."

"Stalking her?"

"She said he came to every show and sat in front and stared at her."

"Isn't that what guys do in those kinds of places?" Brannelly said.

"He was making her uncomfortable. She wanted me to have a word with him."

"Did you?"

"No. It didn't sound like the guy was breaking any laws. I told her I couldn't take the case."

"Did she give you a description of the man?" Brannelly said.

"No. The conversation didn't get that far."

Brannelly stood.

"I'll make a note of it in her file," he said.

"That's it?" Wahlman said. "Seems like—"

"We'll check into it. And I probably don't need to remind you that you shouldn't."

"I wouldn't want to step on anyone's toes," Wahlman said. "But—"

"Then don't," Brannelly said. "Can you find your way back out to the front desk?"

"Sure," Wahlman said.

"Great. Thanks for coming in."

Wahlman exited the suite, nodded to the sergeant at the front desk on his way outside.

Wahlman knew from experience as a law enforcement officer in the Navy that places like Laupin's had a high turnover rate. Which meant that the time to go there and talk to Rokki's coworkers was now. Not two weeks from now, or a month from now, or whenever the homicide detectives assigned to the case got around to it. Not that it was their fault. Not necessarily. Louisville had one of the highest murder rates in the country. The men and women in charge of investigating those crimes were kept busy, all day every day. They could only do so much. And a case involving a woman who made her living dancing in a club probably didn't get top priority.

Wahlman had been sincere when he'd told Brannelly that he didn't want to step on any toes, but he figured it wouldn't hurt to drive over to Laupin's and talk to some of the employees. Maybe get a description of the guy Rokki had told him about. Maybe pass the description on to the police.

Then he would be done with it.

Then he could go out and start looking for a job.

# 6

Wahlman waited in the parking lot until the club opened for business, and then he walked inside. There was an anteroom with black paint and mirrored circles on the walls and framed photos of the dancers and a small rectangular chalkboard. The photos were tasteful. Professional. Like something you might see in a magazine. Rokki's wasn't up there. Maybe they'd taken it down already. Or maybe she'd never had one. The chalkboard said *NEXT SHOW 1:00 PM.*

A set of double doors opened into the main lounge. Throbbing music, strobes, disco balls. There was a long bar with a mirror behind it, and some bistro tables with salt and pepper shakers on them, and booths with curtains you could close for privacy. At the far end of the room, a horseshoe-shaped countertop wrapped around a stage about the size of an average bedroom. Shiny brass poles had been positioned strategically near each corner. Wahlman sat on one of the ringside stools, and thirty seconds later a redhead wearing silvery lace-up stiletto heels and a sparkly blue bathing suit slid in next to him and put her hand on his thigh.

"Want to buy me a drink?" she said.

"I just want to talk to you for a few minutes," Wahlman said.

"I can't sit here unless you buy me a drink."

"How much?"

"Thirty bucks."

Wahlman pulled out his wallet, handed her a twenty and a ten. She walked the money up to the bar, came back carrying a highball glass with some ice in it and a skinny red straw and something clear and bubbly.

"Soda water?" Wahlman said.

She shrugged, pulled the straw out of the drink and dragged the wet end across her tongue.

"What do you want to talk about?" she said.

"Rokki Rhodes," Wahlman said.

She slid the straw back into the drink.

"You a cop?" she said.

"Private investigator," Wahlman said.

He handed her a business card. She looked it over, secured it to her hip with the stretchy band on her bikini bottom.

"I've only been here for a week," she said. "I didn't really know her."

"Who really knew her?"

"There's a girl in the dressing room crying her eyes out. I'm guessing she did."

"What's her name?"

"I don't know. I'm not very good with names."

The double doors swung open and a very large man

walked into the room. He wore jeans and leather work boots and a plaid flannel shirt. Like some kind of lumberjack. He was carrying a *Daily Racing Form* in his left hand. Wahlman guessed him to be in his late twenties or early thirties. Six-two or six-three, forearms like propane tanks. He stopped at the bar and bought a bottle of beer, and then he sat at one of the bistro tables and opened a menu. The redhead glanced over at him and smiled.

"You know that guy?" Wahlman said.

"Never seen him before," the redhead said.

"Could you ask the young lady who's crying her eyes out to come out to the lounge for a few minutes?"

"I don't think she's in any kind of shape to talk right now."

"I just gave you thirty dollars. Could you ask her for me?"

"I need to take care of that guy first," the redhead said. "I'm all alone out here right now."

She sauntered back up to the bar and handed the highball glass back to the bartender. He grabbed a wine carafe that had been loaded with poker chips, shook one out and dropped it into a plastic peanut jar. Someone had written *CALLIE* on a piece of paper and had taped the paper to the jar. Wahlman figured it was the club's way of keeping track of how many drinks each lady sold. He figured Callie would get a percentage at the end of her shift, based on how many chips were in her jar.

The man in the plaid flannel shirt was studying his *Racing Form*, making marks on it with a stubby little golf pencil. Callie walked to the table where he was sitting, slid in next to him and put her hand on his thigh. Wahlman couldn't actually hear what was being said, but he was pretty good at reading lips. And Callie was pretty good at sticking to the script. She asked the guy if he wanted to buy her a drink. He shook his head, told her no thanks, pointed at something on the laminated menu. Callie moved her hand from his leg to his shoulder, leaned in and whispered something into his ear. He shook his head again. Pointed at the menu again. Callie nodded disappointedly, stood and walked back over to the bar. She picked up a tablet computer and started tapping and swiping, probably relaying the food order to a similar device in the kitchen. When she was finished with that, she headed over to the left side of the stage and reached for the knob on a door marked *EMPLOYEES ONLY.* Wahlman thought she was going to go to the dressing room and tell the young lady crying her eyes out that a private investigator wanted to talk to her. But she didn't. Instead, she turned around and walked back over to where Wahlman was sitting.

"That guy was asking about Rokki," she said.

"The guy in the flannel shirt?" Wahlman said.

"Yeah. And who wears a flannel shirt in August, anyway?"

"I don't know," Wahlman said. "What did he say to you about Rokki?"

"He didn't say anything to me," Callie said. "He asked the bartender about her. He wanted to know why her picture wasn't out front anymore."

"What did the bartender tell him?" Wahlman said.

"He told him she doesn't work here anymore," Callie said. "That's it?"

"I guess he figured it was none of the guy's business."

"It was on the news this morning," Wahlman said. "It's no big secret."

"I know. Anyway, I just thought I would tell you."

"Are you sure you've never seen that guy before?"

"I'm sure. But like I said, I've only been here for a week."

She clomped back over to the *EMPLOYEES ONLY* door and exited the lounge. The extreme shoes suddenly seemed like bricks strapped to her feet. Wahlman sat there and stared at the empty stage, wondering if she would take them off when it was time for the show to start. It was hard to imagine anyone trying to dance in those things.

Wahlman waited for a few minutes, and then he moseyed up to the bar. The bartender was cutting a pineapple with a long serrated knife and dropping the wedges into a zippered plastic storage bag. He wore black pants and a black vest and a white shirt and a nametag that said Cliff.

"Can I help you?" he said.

Wahlman pulled out a business card. Cliff made a gesture indicating that his hands were sticky. Wahlman held the card up to where he could see it. Cliff leaned in and squinted, immediately went back to the chunk of pineapple he'd been carving on.

"Did you work last night?" Wahlman said.

"No. I was off."

"The guy in the flannel shirt over there. Is he a regular customer?"

"I've seen him a couple of times."

"Just a couple?"

"We get a hundred guys in here every afternoon, twice as many at night. I don't keep track of who comes and who goes."

Wahlman looked around. So far, he and the man in the plaid flannel shirt were the only customers in the club.

"Where is everyone?" Wahlman said.

"It'll start picking up in a little while," Cliff said.

"Have the police been here yet?"

"A couple of guys came in a while ago, looking for Mr. Laupin."

"Detectives?"

"That's what they said."

"You didn't ask to see their badges?"

"No."

"Did Mr. Laupin talk to them?"

"He's out of town," Cliff said. "Should be back tonight."

Wahlman ordered two beers and walked over to the table where the man in the plaid flannel shirt was sitting. The man was still studying the *Racing* Form. He was punching numbers into a pocket calculator with one hand and making notations with the other. He had dark circles under his eyes and a small adhesive bandage on the left side of his neck.

"Cut yourself shaving?" Wahlman said.

The man in the plaid flannel shirt glanced up and looked Wahlman directly in the eyes.

"Huh?" he said.

"I'm a private investigator," Wahlman said. "I was

wondering if I could talk to you for a minute."

The man in the plaid flannel shirt slid the pencil into his shirt pocket.

"About what?" he said.

"About a young lady named Rokki Rhodes," Wahlman said.

"Apparently she doesn't work here anymore," the man in the plaid flannel shirt said.

"She doesn't work anywhere anymore," Wahlman said. "She was murdered last night."

"She's dead?" the man said.

He seemed genuinely surprised. Wahlman set the beers on the table, climbed onto the stool across from him.

"Did you know her personally?" Wahlman said.

"Is one of those for me?" the man said, gesturing toward the longneck bottles.

"Yes," Wahlman said.

The man reached over and picked up one of the bottles, took a long pull, set it back down on the table.

"I didn't know her," he said.

"She wanted me to have a word with a certain gentleman who'd been—"

"Excuse me," the man in the plaid flannel shirt said. "I'll be right back."

He got up and headed toward the restroom. He started to push the door open, hesitated, turned around and made a beeline for the exit. He still had food coming, and his calculator and marked-up *Racing Form* were still on the table, so Wahlman didn't think he was actually going to leave the club. Maybe he needed to get something out of his car. Maybe he needed to make a phone call.

Wahlman sat there and waited for a couple of minutes, and then he walked outside and checked the parking lot.

The man in the plaid flannel shirt wasn't out there.

The man in the plaid flannel shirt was gone.

# 7

The young lady who'd been crying her eyes out in the dressing room told Wahlman that a big guy who usually wore flannel shirts had been coming in and sitting ringside and staring at Rokki while she was on stage, confirming Wahlman's suspicions that the man in the plaid flannel shirt was the stalker.

But Wahlman didn't think he was the killer.

Wahlman didn't think anyone would be stupid enough to show up at a club and order a beer and plate of food just hours after murdering one of the dancers who worked there.

Then again, it seemed strange that the guy had bolted as soon as Wahlman started asking about Rokki. Maybe the man in the plaid flannel shirt had other things to hide.

Wahlman didn't think he was the killer, but he'd asked Cliff for a couple of the plastic storage bags, and he'd zipped up the items that the man in the plaid flannel shirt had left behind—the calculator and the *Racing Form*—just in case.

The young lady who'd been crying her eyes out had told the police the same thing she'd told Wahlman. Which meant that they knew at least as much as he did. Which was good. It meant that Wahlman wouldn't have to go back to the station again and wait his turn to talk to one of the detectives again. It meant that Wahlman had done as much as he could do without getting in the way of the official investigation. It meant that he needed to step away now and go about his business and let the police go about theirs.

Wahlman felt bad about what had happened to Rokki. But, as it had turned out, taking her case probably wouldn't have changed anything. Because, as it had turned out, the stalker and the killer were probably two different people.

Wahlman climbed into the car that Charlie had loaned him, started the engine and turned on the air conditioner and tried to call Natalie again.

Wahlman didn't like cell phones. He didn't like them, but he carried one now, mostly for his P.I. business, a simple flip phone, technology that had been around close to a hundred years, technology that was less likely to be hacked or tracked than the so-called smart phones that had been all the rage in the early and middle parts of the twenty-first century. Those kinds of phones were still around, but most people didn't bother with them these days, preferring privacy over convenience, preferring to be focused rather than distracted. And the people who did use them weren't allowed to use them in cars, or in their places of employment, for the most part. Not legally, anyway.

Natalie answered on the third ring.

"Where are you?" Wahlman said.

"I'm at home," Natalie said. "Packing some things to take back to the dorm."

"Great. I'll be there in a little while. I'm going to help you take your stuff over there, and then I'm going to need to take the car."

"Why can't I keep it for a while?"

"Because that would only leave your mother and me with one vehicle," Wahlman said. "We've talked about this before."

"I need my own car," Natalie said.

"What for?"

"To go places."

"All of your classes are within walking distance from the dorm. I can take you wherever else you need to go."

Natalie didn't say anything for a few seconds. Wahlman could hear her exhaling through her nostrils.

"Maybe I should just forget about college," she said. "Maybe I should—"

"Maybe you should stop being ridiculous," Wahlman said. "I'll be there in a little while. Okay?"

"Fine."

Natalie disconnected.

Wahlman slid the phone back into his pocket and slid the car into gear and headed for home.

# 8

Janelle Pierce slid her phone into her pocket and slid the car she'd rented into gear and headed for home.

Her real home.

In Jeffersonville, Indiana.

It was supposed to have been a surprise visit, but the word had gotten out, as it always did. Now her parents—and the rest of the world—knew she was coming. And thanks to a certain entertainment columnist who seemed downright obsessed with Janelle, they even knew why. Not that it would have taken a great deal of imagination to figure it out. Not if you knew that Janelle owned a thoroughbred named T. J. Ricochet, and not if you knew that T. J. Ricochet would be running in the fifth race at River City Downs this evening.

Now Janelle wouldn't be able to spend the night in her old room, as she'd originally planned to do, because spending the night in her old room meant that a hundred or more people would be standing on her parents' front lawn by morning. Friends from grade school, and friends of *friends* from grade school, and the paparazzi, and other complete strangers who seemed to think that it was perfectly acceptable to invade your privacy on a regular basis just because you were a major hit at the box office. Just because you made more money last year than most people will make in a lifetime.

All of the attention was silly, and annoying, but it had somehow become the norm for Janelle, and she figured she might as well get used to it. She figured it wasn't likely to go away anytime soon.

She steered out of the hotel parking lot and took the ramp to the interstate. Traffic was heavy around the airport, but it started to clear as she made her way downtown and across the bridge to Indiana. Once she made it to the Jeffersonville exit, it was smooth sailing all the way to her parents' driveway.

Janelle had offered to move her parents to California, to buy them a house out there, but they had refused, saying that this was their home, that this was where they intended to stay for the rest of their lives. The house was modest, but nice, three bedrooms and two baths with a big kitchen and a living room and a den, everything recently updated, inside and out, thanks to Janelle, who'd also insisted on paying off the mortgage. Now her dad worked sixty hours a week because he wanted to, not because he had to.

Her mother stepped out onto the porch. Janelle climbed out of the SUV and trotted to where she was standing and gave her a hug.

"So good to see you," her mother said. "How was your flight?"

31

"It was good."

"First class?"

"Yes, Mom. First class."

"Well, you can afford it."

"I suppose," Janelle said, staring down at the painted concrete.

"You should never be embarrassed about how successful you've become," her mother said.

"I'm not embarrassed," Janelle said. "Not exactly. But sometimes I think about how many homeless people a ticket like that could feed."

"You've given a lot of money to a lot of charities. You've helped a lot of people. I'm very proud of you."

"Thanks."

Her mother gestured toward the SUV.

"That's a nice car you rented," she said.

"It cost a bundle too," Janelle said. "But I figured you and Dad would want to go to Louisville with me this evening, and I wanted everyone to be comfortable."

"Oh, yes, we definitely want to go. It's all your father has been talking about. We can't wait!"

"Is Dad home?" Janelle said.

"He's still at work," her mother said. "But he's taking off early today. Should be home soon. Come on in and I'll fix you something to eat."

"I had a soda and some French fries a while ago. So I'm really not very—"

"That's not a meal. I'm going to fix you something decent. Come on."

Janelle followed her mother across the porch and through the front door and into the foyer. As soon as she stepped inside, she could tell by the wonderful aroma that her mother had been baking something for dessert.

Apple pie.

Janelle's favorite.

# 9

In 1983, seventy-four years before Rock Wahlman was born, a United States Army officer named Jack Reacher was transported to an Air Force base in Germany and treated for injuries sustained during an attack in Lebanon. Based on his own experiences in such settings, Wahlman imagined that Reacher had been in a lot of pain, and that the hospital food had sucked, and that it had been difficult to get any rest, with multiple doctors and nurses and other staff members marching into the ward and poking and prodding and asking questions around the clock.

Based on what Wahlman had been told, and backed by some of the research he'd conducted, one of the Army phlebotomists had stepped up to Reacher's bed and had tied a tourniquet around his arm and had drawn some blood one morning, just like one of the Army phlebotomists had done every morning there at the hospital in Germany, only this time, unbeknownst to Reacher, the Army phlebotomist had drawn an extra redtop, a vial that was shipped, along with thirty-nine other vials from thirty-nine other military patients, to a secret underground laboratory in Colorado. The samples were analyzed, and then they were cryogenically preserved.

Decades later, a group of independent scientists had gotten the greenlight—from the three-star general who'd been in charge of the lab at the time—to use the specimens for a top secret and altogether illegal human cloning experiment. While a total of eighty fetuses were produced, only two survived, both of them grown from cells taken from the officer named Reacher. The Army ended up bailing on the project and the babies were given fake identities and fake backstories and sent to separate orphanages in separate states.

Wahlman had been one of those babies.

He was thinking about all of that as he steered into his driveway on Fifth Street. He didn't have a father, or a mother who was actually related to him. No blood relatives of any kind, except for the other clone, who was dead now, murdered by a rogue pair of senior Army officers who'd tried to kill Wahlman as well.

All in the name of *progress.*

Or, more specifically, in the name of the billions of privately-pledged research dollars that would supposedly lead to the so-called progress.

Rock Wahlman was an exact genetic duplicate of Jack Reacher, which meant that the only family history he would ever have to go on was Jack Reacher's family history, and he didn't really know much about it. He wanted to know more. He was going to be forty-four years old soon. Maybe there were medical issues that he needed to be aware of. Maybe there were other issues.

Natalie walked out to the driveway as he was climbing out of the car.

"Cool!" she said. "Did you buy this?"

"I borrowed it from Charlie," Wahlman said. "I have to take it back this evening."

"You should just go ahead and buy it from him."

"You think so?"

"Yeah. You should buy it from him and then give it to me."

"Keep dreaming," Wahlman said.

"Can I at least drive it around the block?"

"Better not. Got all your stuff packed yet?"

"Most of it," Natalie said. "I can't believe I'm going to be stuck on campus with no transportation."

"More time for studying," Wahlman said. "I've been thinking about taking some classes myself. Maybe we could meet at the library sometimes and—"

"Please tell me you're not serious," Natalie said.

Wahlman laughed.

"Don't worry," he said. "Even if I do take some classes, I won't make you study with me. Come on. Let's start loading your stuff into the car."

"I talked to Mom a while ago." Natalie said.

"You did?"

"Yeah. She told me about your client. Or your almost-client, or whatever. Does she really look like Janelle Pierce?"

Apparently Natalie hadn't heard the news. Wahlman

wondered if he should tell her. He decided that he might as well. She was going to hear about it eventually anyway.

"They found her in the park this morning," he said. "She's dead."

"Janelle Pierce?"

"No. My almost-client."

"What happened?"

"Someone stabbed her to death."

"That's terrible," Natalie said. "Do they know who did it?"

"Not yet," Wahlman said. "Let's get your stuff loaded."

Natalie turned and started walking toward the porch.

"She's in town," she said. "Did you know that?"

"Who?" Wahlman said.

"Janelle Pierce. The real Janelle Pierce. That's what I heard, anyway."

"What else did you hear?"

"Nothing. Just that she might be at the track tonight."

"Churchill Downs?"

"River City. I think she owns one of the horses racing over there."

Wahlman's heart skipped a beat. Everything that had happened over the past twenty-four hours started swirling through his head like a plaid flannel tornado.

"Go on inside," he said. "I'll be there shortly."

Natalie walked inside. Wahlman opened the driver side door of the car he'd borrowed, reached in and grabbed the plastic bag with the *Daily Racing Form* in it. He unzipped the bag and pulled the paper out and frantically started shuffling through the pages.

It took him a couple of minutes to find the horse. The column had been circled in pencil, several times, and some notations had been scribbled into the margins.

T. J. Ricochet.

A filly. Scheduled to run in the fifth race at River City Downs today.

And the race was scheduled to start in ten minutes.

Wahlman trotted up the sidewalk and slung the front door open and told Natalie that he wasn't going to be able to help her move her stuff after all.

# 10

Janelle steered into the parking area that was reserved for owners and trainers, stopped at the security shack and presented her official River City Downs identification badge to the guy at the window. The guy handed her a laminated parking pass to hang on her rearview mirror and told her to have a nice day. She found a place to park and switched the engine off, and then she and her parents climbed out and started walking toward the stables.

"We need to hurry," Janelle said. "The race starts in a few minutes."

"Smells like horse shit back here," her father said.

"What do you expect?" her mother said, laughing.

A few feet beyond the stables, there was a walkway that branched off in several different directions. You could go to the grandstands or the clubhouse and mingle with the general admission crowd, or you could go to the handling area and mingle with the jockeys and the trainers, or—if you were fabulously wealthy—you could swipe your official River City Downs identification badge and press your finger

39

against the little glass window on the fingerprint scanner and take the stairs to the private suites on the second level and mingle with nobody.

Janelle veered toward the stairs.

"You rented a suite?" her father said. "How much did that set you back?"

Janelle started to answer. She started to say that it was a lot, but that it was worth every penny for the peace of mind, for the added security and privacy. She started to say that, but before the words actually left her mouth, she noticed a man standing at the foot of the stairwell.

The closer she got to the man, the more familiar he looked.

It couldn't be.

But it was.

Not a friend from grade school this time, but from high school.

And not just a friend, but her boyfriend. Her high school sweetheart.

Junior and senior years.

Her date to every event, every ballgame, every dance.

An expression of great surprise washed across his face when he saw her coming. She walked up to him and gave him a hug, a loose and quick and rather unaffectionate one, the kind that couldn't possibly be mistaken for anything other than what it was, the kind you feel obligated to give to an acquaintance you'd actually hoped never to see again.

Marshall had put on a little weight since high school, all of it muscle. Leaning into his chest and abdomen was like leaning into a brick wall.

"What are you doing here?" Janelle said.

"I was just about to ask you the same thing," he said.

"Mom, Dad, you remember Marshall."

"Of course," Janelle's mother said, stepping forward to shake Marshall's hand.

Janelle's father did not step forward to shake Marshall's hand. Janelle's father had never liked Marshall, and he'd never pretended to like him.

"We were just on our way upstairs," Janelle said. "Kind of in a hurry, to tell you the truth. But it was nice to—"

"Isn't this a restricted area?" Janelle's father said, glaring at Marshall in a manner similar to the way he'd glared at him when Janelle was still a teenager.

"I was up in the clubhouse, decided to walk around a little bit," Marshall said. "Must have taken a wrong turn."

"Are you here by yourself?" Janelle's mother said.

"Yes, ma'am."

"You should join us upstairs in our suite for a while. That would be okay, wouldn't it, Janelle?"

Janelle shrugged.

"Sure," she said, glancing over at her father and noticing how clenched his jaw had become and how red his face had gotten and wishing once again that she and her parents had never run into Marshall in the first place.

"I wouldn't want to impose," Marshall said.

"Nonsense," Janelle's mother said. "Come on up. At least for one drink. Janelle's horse is running in a few minutes. Did you know that?"

"I didn't know that," Marshall said. "How exciting."

Janelle swiped her badge and pressed her right index finger on the scanner and led the way through the computer-controlled security gate. Maybe this wouldn't be so bad, she thought. Maybe Marshall really would just have one drink and then head on back to the clubhouse.

Janelle thought about the very last night that she and Marshall were together.

The relationship hadn't ended well.

It hadn't ended well at all.

Marshall had a temper, and it had gotten progressively worse during the years that Janelle had been with him. He'd never actually hit Janelle, but he'd been verbally abusive, and he'd broken some things, and Janelle had figured that it was just a matter of time until he snapped. She'd walked away from him on graduation night, making it clear that it was over and that she was moving on.

The relentless onslaught of phone calls and text messages that followed were not exactly unexpected, but horrifying nonetheless.

If Janelle's mother ever found out about some of the things that Marshall had said to Janelle back then, she would probably never speak to him again.

If Janelle's father ever found out about some of the things that Marshall had said to Janelle back then, he would probably kill him.

Janelle tried not to think about it.

Her mother said something to Marshall on the way up the stairs—teasing him a bit, but in a playful, lighthearted way. Something about the shirt he was wearing. She'd always found it amusing that he liked flannel so much, even in the summer.

# 11

River City Downs had opened for business in 2075, exactly two hundred years after the opening of the most famous thoroughbred racetrack in the world. It was fancy and modern and expensive. It was a nice place to spend an afternoon and a paycheck. Wahlman steered into the parking area that was reserved for owners and trainers, screeched to a stop at the security shack and spoke to the guy at the window.

"I'm looking for Janelle Pierce," Wahlman said.

The guard laughed.

"You and about a million other people," he said.

The guard wore khaki pants and a khaki shirt. His nametag said Moffit. There was a walkie-talkie clipped to his patent leather belt and a silver badge pinned to his left breast pocket. He didn't appear to be armed.

"Is she here somewhere?" Wahlman said.

"I'm not at liberty to say," Moffit said. "Is there something else I can help you with? If not, I'm going to have to ask you to—"

"I have reason to believe that her life might be in danger," Wahlman said.

"Are you a police officer?"

"I'm a private investigator."

Moffit laughed again.

"You and about a million other people," he said again.

Wahlman gripped the steering wheel tightly, made a concerted effort not to lean into the guard shack window and grip Moffit's throat.

"I don't have time to explain," Wahlman said. "Is Ms. Pierce somewhere here at the track, or not?"

"Again, I'm not at liberty to say."

"Which pretty much tells me that she's here," Wahlman said. "If she wasn't, you would just say no."

Moffit shrugged.

"You can think whatever you want to think," he said.

"I need to find her," Wahlman said. "Or at least talk to her. I know she's here. Is there any way you could call her on the phone?"

"There's a car behind you," Moffit said. "I'm going to need you to pull forward and pull over to the right."

"Then what?"

"Then I'm going to take care of the gentleman behind you. Then I'm going to call the security office and let my supervisor know that we have a problem. Then my supervisor is going to come out here and talk to you, and there's a good chance that you'll be escorted from the property. And if you resist in any way, shape, or form, there's a good chance—and I mean a very good chance—that my supervisor will notify the Louisville Police Department and let them deal with you."

Wahlman checked his rearview mirror. There was indeed a car behind him. A very fat car with a very fat man in the driver seat, a man with curly gray hair and a mustache, tapping his fingers impatiently on the dashboard.

"How long is it going to take to get your supervisor out here?" Wahlman said.

"Not long."

"Make the call. Make it now."

"I'll make the call when I'm ready to make the call," Moffit said. "Pull forward and pull over to the right. We'll be with you shortly. I promise."

Wahlman didn't pull forward and pull over to the right. Instead, he switched off the ignition and climbed out of the car and stepped around to the front of the guard shack and kicked the door in.

"This is an urgent situation," he said. "Maybe I didn't make that clear."

The guard reached for the phone. Wahlman took a step forward and clouted him in the forehead with a closed fist, knowing that such an action could potentially end his career as a private investigator, especially if he was wrong about Janelle Pierce's life being in danger.

But he was almost certain that he wasn't wrong. He was betting everything he'd worked for over the past three years on it. He was almost certain that the guy in the plaid flannel shirt had killed Rokki Rhodes, and he was almost certain that the same guy was now planning to kill Janelle Pierce.

He didn't know why the guy wanted to kill Janelle, or why he'd wanted to kill her lookalike. He couldn't imagine a motive, but it was too much of a coincidence that the guy had been stalking Rokki one day and showing a great interest in Janelle's racehorse the next. In Wahlman's experience, coincidences weren't really coincidences most of the time. They were the results of deliberate acts.

Moffit's eyes rolled back in his head and he crumpled to the floor. Wahlman made sure that he was still alive, and then he stepped over to the desk and checked the logbook. Which, similar to the system that the United States Navy used for watch duty and quarterdeck activity and other potentially important notations, was an actual physical book, with lined pages and entries written neatly in black ink. Computers were great for a lot of things, but even the tightest and most expensive digital networks were subject to attack. When you wanted to be absolutely certain that some bonehead down the street—or on the other side of the world—wasn't watching your every move, the old ways were still the best ways.

Wahlman found the entry he was looking for.

Tamara Janelle Pierce, owner of a two-year-old filly named T.J. Ricochet, had been granted access to the V.I.P. parking area at 15:37, along with two guests, one male and one female.

And that was all that Moffit had written. There was no indication of where Janelle and her guests had gone after they'd gotten out of their car.

Wahlman looked around for a list of phone numbers. He

didn't know for sure, but he figured that someone as famous as Janelle Pierce would insist on a private suite. They were extremely expensive, but Janelle was one of the highest paid actresses in the world. She could afford it. Wahlman figured he could call every suite until he found the right one. Until Janelle or one of her guests answered the phone. But there was no list. No hardcopy, anyway. In-house phone listings were a lot different than actual log entries, which often included sensitive personal information. In-house phone numbers were of little use to hackers. They were probably kept in a file on the computer, easily accessible from any station in the network. Again, the way the Navy did it.

Wahlman stepped over to the desk and pressed one of the keys on the keyboard. The monitor blinked on and a pair of login boxes appeared on the screen, one for a user name and one for a password.

Which meant that Wahlman was going to have to think of something else.

He was thinking about grabbing Moffit's walkie-talkie and keying the transmitter and pretending to be Moffit and trying to get the phone number to Janelle's suite from whoever answered on the other end when he glanced out the window and saw three more uniformed guards running toward the shack.

# 12

T.J. Ricochet did not win.

Or place.

Or show.

"Good thing we didn't bet a lot of money on that horse," Janelle's father said.

"She'll do better next time," her mother said.

Janelle poured herself another drink. Vodka on the rocks. Her fourth. She looked over at Marshall and gestured questioningly toward the bar.

"No thanks," he said. "I really need to get going."

Janelle set her drink down, stepped over and gave him a hug.

Another loose and quick one.

"Nice seeing you," she said. "Take care of yourself."

Marshall leaned down and whispered in her ear.

"Can I talk to you for a minute?" he said. "In private?"

Janelle wanted for this little chance meeting to be over as soon as possible. She had no interest in talking to Marshall, in private or otherwise. She had no interest in talking to him, but she didn't want to be rude to him in front of her mother, and she certainly didn't want to make him angry. She knew from experience that his personality could change in a heartbeat. There was no reason to risk creating that sort of scene.

She backed away and turned toward her parents.

"I'm going to walk Marshall out to his car," she said. "Be right back."

Marshall told Janelle's mother and father how nice it had been to see them. Janelle's mother smiled and said likewise. Janelle's father grunted and turned toward the window to watch the horses walk to the gate for the next race.

Janelle followed Marshall out to the hallway. She walked beside him on the way to the stairs, keeping her arms folded across her chest, hoping he wouldn't try to hold her hand or put his arm around her. She was starting to think that the uninviting body language was going to be enough, and that this was going to be over soon, and that everything was going to be okay, when Marshall reached over and put his hand on her shoulder.

"Why didn't you ever return my calls?" he said.

Janelle stopped walking.

"Maybe this wasn't such a good idea," she said. "I'm going to go on back to the suite now. You take care of yourself, okay?"

"All I ever wanted was to love you."

"It was high school. It was a long time ago. People change. People move on. That's just the way it is."

"I still love you. I've never stopped loving you."

"Marshall—"

"Why can't you give me another chance?"

"I need to go now," Janelle said. "It was good seeing you, but I need to go."

Marshall reached under the tails of his flannel shirt and pulled out a semi-automatic pistol and pointed it directly at Janelle's face. A chill washed over her and her knees got weak and her heart felt as though it was going to thump its way out of her chest.

"We're going to walk to your car," Marshall said. "We're going to do it slowly and calmly, as if absolutely nothing is wrong. If you scream, or shout, or try to run away—"

"You're insane, Marshall. You need help."

"I need you to shut your mouth and move on down the stairs."

"You're never going to get away with this. You know that, right? My parents are—"

"Move. I'll be right behind you."

# 13

The fat guy in the fat car was gone. He must have called the security office, and then he must have backed out of the V.I.P. lane and headed over to one of the general admission lots, hoping to avoid the kinds of misunderstandings and subsequent conflicts that sometimes ensued when an angry motorist climbed out of a sleek and speedy two-seater and walked around to the front of a guard shack and viciously splintered the doorframe with the heel of a size-fourteen work boot.

Two of the private security officers currently running toward the shack appeared to be unarmed. Like Moffit. The only things clipped to their belts were keyrings and walkie-talkies. They were chubby and slow, and Wahlman didn't think they would pose much of a problem.

The third guard, however, the one leading the pack, the one out in front by a good twenty feet or so, was a different story. He was lean and fast and muscular and appeared to be packing a pistol and a stun gun and some sort of grenade—smoke, or tear gas—along with an expandable baton and a pair of handcuffs. He stopped a few feet from the shack and pulled his pistol out of its holster and dropped to one knee and aimed toward the window and waited for Chubby Guard One and Chubby Guard Two to catch up.

"Lace your fingers behind your head and step out of the shack," the lean and muscular guard shouted.

"I'm trying to save someone's life," Wahlman shouted in return.

"Come on out and we'll talk about it."

Wahlman thought it over for a few seconds, decided to comply with the guard's orders. Decided that he didn't have much of a choice. He laced his fingers behind his head, stepped over to the ruined door and swung it open with his foot.

And was promptly met with a crushing blow to the side of his neck.

The expandable nightstick, he thought, as the pain swept through his body and the fireworks exploded in his head. His knees crumpled and a fist or a foot or a sledgehammer or something slammed against the center of his chest and he was suddenly inside the shack again, staring at the ceiling. Chubby Guard One jumped on top of him and straddled his torso and punched him in the face while the lean and muscular guard slapped the cuffs on his wrists.

"That's enough," the lean and muscular guard said. "Get him up to the chair."

Chubby Guard One and Chubby Guard Two got Wahlman up to the chair. All six feet four inches and two hundred and forty pounds of him. It was a struggle. Chubby

Guard One and Chubby Guard Two were breathing hard by the time they finished the assignment. Chubby Guard Two looked like he might throw up.

Moffit was still on the floor. He was still unconscious. There was a bump on his forehead where Wahlman had clobbered him.

Chubby Guard One crouched down and checked him for a pulse.

"He's going to need some attention," he said.

"The police and an ambulance are on the way," the lean and muscular guard said. "We're going to sit here quietly until they arrive."

"Are you the supervisor?" Wahlman said.

"Yes. My name is Lancaster."

"You're name's going to be dog shit if you don't listen closely to what I'm going to tell you and do exactly as I say."

Lancaster laughed.

"Breaking and entering. Assault and battery. You're in a lot of trouble, my friend. I don't think you're in any position to—"

"Just shut up and listen," Wahlman shouted.

But Lancaster didn't shut up and listen. Instead, he whipped out the expandable baton and smacked Wahlman on the thigh with it, smacked him hard, with great force, as if he were trying to swat some sort of flying pest. A fresh jolt of agony traveled up the left side of Wahlman's body, searing a pathway through his jawbone and up to the tip of his scalp.

"What part of *quietly* did you not understand?" Lancaster said.

Wahlman breathed in through his teeth, tried to huff some of the pain away.

"There's a very good chance that a young lady is going to die this afternoon," he said. "And if she does, it's going to be your fault. You can either stand there and beat me to death with that thing, or you can—"

Something outside of the shack caught Wahlman's eye.

Something about a hundred feet from the window.

A man and a woman. Walking toward an SUV. They were too far away for Wahlman to make out their facial features, but there was no mistake about the shirt the man was wearing.

No mistake whatsoever.

"They're out there," Wahlman said. "They're getting into a car. Surely you're not going to just sit here and—"

Lancaster smacked him with the baton again. Same leg. Same spot.

After fighting off a wave of nausea for a few seconds, and after several more seconds of careful consideration, Wahlman came to the conclusion that any further conversation with Lancaster would be a waste of time. Therefore, he didn't say anything as he leaned back in the desk chair and kicked the security supervisor's right kneecap with approximately the same force as he'd used on the door earlier. Lancaster shouted out in pain and fell to the floor and reached for his pistol. Wahlman stood and stomped on his face until he stopped reaching.

Chubby Guard One and Chubby Guard Two came at Wahlman and grabbed him by the arms and tried to wrestle him to the floor. Which was a big mistake on their part. They should have kept their distance. They should have exited the shack immediately, and then they should have used their walkie-talkies to call for help. Maybe this would be a learning experience for them, Wahlman thought. Maybe they would be smarter next time. Probably not, but it was possible. At any rate, they came at him and grabbed him by the arms and he quickly put one of them down with a knee to the ribs and the other with an elbow to the jaw, and then he crouched down and grabbed the stun gun from Lancaster's holster and made sure that neither of them would bother him while he hunted for the keys to the handcuffs.

# 14

Marshall kept the pistol aimed at Janelle's core as he steered the SUV through the parking complex and out to the main thoroughfare. He'd locked the controls on the doors and windows, so there was no way for Janelle to escape, even if a momentary diversion from outside of the car caused a momentary lapse in concentration on Marshall's part. Even if some other kind of unforeseen opportunity presented itself. Her only hope was that Marshall really wasn't as crazy as he seemed to be, that it was all just an act, an extreme and misguided effort at winning back her love.

"Where are we going?" she said.

"Does it matter?" Marshall said.

"I know you're not going to kill me. That's just not who you are."

"Like you said, people change."

"You're just trying to scare me," Janelle said. "Well, it's working. I'm scared. You've accomplished what you set out to accomplish. So put the gun away and—"

"We had something special," Marshall said. "Or at least I thought we did. But I guess people like me don't matter anymore, since you're a bigtime movie star now."

"That's not it. That's not it at all."

"Then what is it? You loved me before. Why can't you love me now?"

Janelle couldn't love Marshall now for the same reason she couldn't love him eleven years ago. Because he was an asshole. An abusive jerk with a short fuse and a total disregard for other people's feelings.

But of course she didn't tell him that. She didn't want to antagonize him, didn't want the situation to get more out of hand than it already was.

"I just don't think we're right for each other," she said. "It doesn't mean that you're a bad person, or that I'm a bad person, or that—"

"Shut up," Marshall said.

Janelle glanced down at the gun. Marshall's hand was trembling. He was nervous. His finger was on the trigger. One hiccup and a large-caliber bullet would bore a large-caliber tunnel through Janelle's ribcage. She hoped that one of the tires on the SUV didn't hit a bump or sink into a pothole or something.

"You need to let it go," she said. "You need to move on. Turn around and take me back to the track right now, and we can forget that any of this ever happened."

Marshall didn't say anything. And he didn't turn around. He kept driving and he kept pointing the gun at Janelle, and she suddenly realized where they were going.

To the park.

Where it had started, and where it had ended, all those years ago.

# 15

Janelle didn't feel right. She'd consumed quite a bit of alcohol, but that wasn't it. She could hold her liquor with the best of them. This was different. Some kind of drug. Marshall must have slipped something into one of her drinks back at the track. Everything seemed more vivid than usual. More colorful. Bright squiggly lines made their way from one side of her visual field to the other. Like tiny psychedelic worms. She tried to blink them away, but it was no use. Maybe the drug would wear off soon. She hoped that it would.

She still didn't think that Marshall was planning to kill her. She just didn't think that he had it in him.

Then she saw the traffic barricades and the crime scene tape blocking the turnoff to the second lookout.

"Wonder what happened up there?" she said.

"I thought you would have heard by now," Marshall said.

"Heard what?"

"Nothing. It's not important."

"No, really. What happened?"

"A young lady was murdered late last night," Marshall said. "Right here in the park."

"You're kidding," Janelle said, knowing of course that he wasn't.

"She was a stripper," Marshall said. "And you know what they said about her on the news this morning?"

"What?"

"They said she looked a lot like you. In fact, the guy who found her thought that she was you. Crazy, huh?"

Janelle glanced down at the pistol again. The tip of the barrel was jittering like a needle on a pressure gauge. Marshall's face was slick with sweat, even though he'd cranked the air conditioner up to its highest setting.

"You shot her?" Janelle said. "Is that what you want me to believe?"

Marshall smiled. It seemed as though he was trying to stifle a laugh.

"I didn't shoot her," he said.

Janelle's throat tightened. Marshall's behavior was getting more and more bizarre. Maybe he really was planning to kill her.

"I'll give you whatever you want," she said. "I'll give you a million dollars. Just let me go."

"I don't want your money," Marshall said. "You think you can just buy me, like you buy everyone else? I loved you. I wanted to spend the rest of my life with you. All those promises we made. They didn't mean a thing to you, did they?"

"Maybe we can work things out," Janelle said. "Let's go

back to the track and talk it over."

Marshall didn't try to hold it back this time. He laughed. Hard.

"It's way too late for anything like that," he said. "I might be stupid, but I'm not *that* stupid."

"It's not too late. I won't say anything to anyone. I promise."

"I know you're not going to say anything to anyone," Marshall said. "I know that for sure. That's one promise that you're definitely going to keep."

Marshall turned onto the road that led to the third lookout. Maybe there would be people, Janelle thought. There usually were people up there in the summer, during daylight hours. Maybe there would be another group of teenagers, goofing off, like there had been down at the first lookout, where Marshall had stopped earlier. Maybe there would be runners, and cyclists, and sweethearts walking hand-in-hand, enjoying the panoramic view of the city as they navigated the perimeter, maybe stopping and pointing out the various landmarks you could see from the edge of the cliff, maybe even trying to find their own houses, their own tiny specks of real estate in the distance. Maybe there would be families with lawn chairs and buckets of fried chicken and two-liter bottles of soda.

Maybe there would be people.

And maybe Janelle would scream for help this time.

Scream for help, knowing that it might be the last thing she ever did.

# 16

The sleek and speedy two-seater that Wahlman had borrowed from Charlie had been built by hand in a tiny factory on a tiny island off the coast of France. All electric, with solar panels and magnetic turbines and cyclic wind generators—all of which greatly reduced the need for plugging in and charging. Advertisements for the vehicle claimed that it could take you from zero to sixty in 1.4 seconds, while saving you a bundle in energy costs at the same time.

Wahlman had been somewhat skeptical about the acceleration metrics until he fishtailed out of the parking lot and floored the pedal and shot forward like a missile out of a cannon. It was the kind of power that could quickly get away from you if you weren't careful. The kind that could get you in trouble with the law. The kind that could get you killed.

Wahlman eased off the accelerator, kept the top speed at around ninety. He took a right on Third, and then he veered onto Southern Parkway, thinking that the man in the plaid flannel shirt might be taking Janelle Pierce to the same place he'd taken Rokki Rhodes—to one of the lookouts up in the park.

Reevaluating as he traveled along, figuring that any sort of encounter with the police would result in immediate and prolonged detainment, he slowed down some more, but he still made it to the intersection of Southern Parkway and Newcut Road in a little under five minutes.

A pair of Louisville Police Department cruisers were blocking the main entrance to the park. Nose-to-nose, strobes flashing. Wahlman wondered if the entire area was being treated as a crime scene. Not because of Janelle. It was way too soon for that. Because of Rokki. Because of what had happened earlier.

If the entire park—all 739 acres of it—was being treated as a crime scene, then the man in the plaid flannel shirt would have been forced to take Janelle somewhere else. And if that was the case, there wasn't much more that Wahlman could do. He had no idea where else to look. He supposed he would need to head back downtown and explain the situation to Brannelly or one of the other homicide detectives and hope that they didn't arrest him for what had happened at River City Downs.

He waited at the traffic light and took a left and noticed some kids swinging on the swings and some players playing on the tennis courts. Which meant that the park was open. Which was good. It meant that Janelle might still have a chance.

Wahlman raced down to the south entrance and saw that

it was accessible and he swung in and steered past the parking area and around to the amphitheater and up toward the golf course.

Iroquois Park was basically just a very large hill, a massive elevation in a part of town that was otherwise relatively flat. The road that led to the top was curvy, and there weren't any guardrails. You had to watch your speed, even in a car that handled as well as the two-seater. If you didn't, there was a good chance that you would skid off the edge and maybe roll like a barrel and maybe go airborne for a couple of seconds and maybe end up skewered on a tree branch down in one of the gulches.

Wahlman strongly preferred for that not to happen, so he third-geared it most of the way to the first lookout, where a group of teenagers were hanging out, smoking cigarettes and throwing Frisbees and riding skateboards.

A rock and mortar barrier, two and a half or three feet tall, skirted the perimeter of the viewing area. One of the boys was sitting there with one of the girls. Kissing and hugging, carrying on as if they were the only two people on the planet. Wahlman figured they were about fifteen. Maybe sixteen. He remembered being that age and being in love and doing the same kind of thing and not caring what anyone thought about it. He also remembered Natalie being that age, and he remembered advising her to stay away from boys until she turned thirty. He'd been joking, of course, but he figured the basic message had gotten through.

He steered the car over to where the couple was sitting and rolled the window down and asked if they'd seen anyone driving a white SUV with tinted windows. The girl looked embarrassed. She didn't say anything. The boy told Wahlman that there had been a car like that parked there earlier, but that it had driven away shortly after he and his friends had arrived.

"Thanks," Wahlman said. "Stay in school, and stay away from drugs and alcohol, and practice safe sex."

"Huh?" the boy said.

"Just do the right thing."

The girl looked embarrassed some more. The boy shrugged. Wahlman drove on.

He continued up the hill, passing a series of reflective road signs reminding motorists and cyclists and pedestrians that deer were crossing and rocks were falling and cell phone reception was poor. Wahlman had never heard of any rocks falling on anyone, but just last week he'd read an article about a guy who'd swerved to miss a doe and her fawn and had ended up deep in the woods, trapped in his car and unable to call for help. His wife had reported him missing, and a search team had been sent out, and they'd found him in time, but just barely. The top of the park was a pretty dangerous place to be, even when you weren't looking for a suspected murderer and a world-renowned movie star who was potentially going to be his next victim.

A row of orange and white traffic barricades—joined together with strips of yellow crime scene tape—blocked the turnoff to the second lookout. Where the hiker had found Rokki Rhodes, Wahlman thought. He figured that the area would be closed to the public for several days. Several weeks, maybe.

He continued toward the top, toward the third and final lookout. When he got there, he steered over to the edge and shut the engine off and climbed out of the car. The rock and mortar barrier was slightly taller than the one down at the first lookout, and there was a lip at the bottom that had probably been added as an extra safety measure. Mostly for nighttime visitors, Wahlman thought, a little wall about the height of a stair step that a tire would run into, theoretically preventing the entire vehicle from crashing through and sailing past the treetops and arcing on down to the rocky creek bed below.

Wahlman stood there and gazed out over the valley. The city seemed a million miles away. The sky was blue and the trees were green and there was nobody else around. No teenagers. No white SUV. Nobody.

Ordinarily, Wahlman would have enjoyed the serenity. The peace and quiet. But the fact that nobody else was around possibly meant that his hunch about the man in the plaid flannel shirt was wrong. Maybe the man was just an old friend or something. Maybe he hadn't killed Rokki Rhodes, and maybe he wasn't planning to kill Janelle Pierce.

Wahlman didn't even know for sure that Janelle was with the man. He'd seen someone who fit her general description climb into the SUV with him, but he hadn't been close enough to make a positive identification. And everything else had been guesswork. Maybe Wahlman had been wrong about everything.

He was considering that possibility when he heard a series of muffled grunts somewhere down in the woods.

# 17

Marshall hadn't driven the SUV all the way up to the third lookout. He'd switched on the four-wheel-drive and had steered off the edge of the blacktop into the thick and lush foliage that covered the undeveloped parts of the park this time of the year. He'd forced Janelle to stuff one of her socks in her mouth, and then he'd pulled a pair of nylon cable ties out of his pocket and had used them to secure her wrists and ankles.

Now she was on the ground, staring up at the vines and leaves and branches, grunting frantically, totally helpless.

She felt as though she might pass out any second, might succumb to the thick August heat and the outrageous assault on her mind and body. She was about to close her eyes and give into it when she noticed a hornet's nest the size of a watermelon dangling from one of the tree limbs, twenty feet or so above the top of the SUV.

Bees terrified Janelle. They were her only true phobia. In any sort of ordinary situation, the sight of the nest would have caused her to experience extreme anxiety. Sweaty palms, heart palpitations, shortness of breath—a genuine panic attack. But ironically, in the current situation, which was by far the direst that Janelle had ever been forced to endure, the sight of the nest seemed to provide a calming effect. Maybe it was the bluish gray color. Or the incessant hum. Or the oddly-shaped specks of sunshine breaking through the canopy and beaming down on it, the effect reminding Janelle of a giant prehistoric egg she'd seen in a painting one time. Maybe it was the power, or the illusion of power, the wavy strands of hot blue electrical current that seemed to surround the nest. Whatever it was, Janelle decided to make it her own. She decided to latch onto it and try to use it as a psychological shield, a reprieve from the horror for as long as she was able to remain conscious.

Marshall tossed the pistol onto the driver seat, and then he produce a pocketknife, the kind with a single blade that locked in place when you opened it all the way. He crouched down and pulled the front of Janelle's shirt up and pressed the point of the blade against her skin, an inch or so to the left of her bellybutton.

"See?" he said, laughing nervously. "I was telling you the truth about Rokki. I didn't shoot her. And I'm not going to shoot you. Gunshots attract too much attention. You can hear them for miles. People would wonder. Anyone nearby might get curious, try to follow the sound. And of course there's quite a police presence here in the park today. It wouldn't take long for one of those cruisers down at the main entrance to drive up here and start looking around. Best to stay quiet, wouldn't you say?"

Janelle didn't look at Marshall. She didn't plead with her eyes. Shrieks and moans didn't erupt from the deepest part of her chest, as they had just minutes ago. She'd decided to rewrite the script. She'd decided to approach the role of *woman in jeopardy* in a totally different way. She'd decided that she was no longer going to feed Marshall's insanity. She wasn't going to give him the satisfaction of watching her squirm.

She stared at the big blue electric egg, breathed in through her nose and out through her mouth and felt more relaxed than she'd ever felt in her entire life.

She didn't flinch.

Or cry.

Even when the tip of the blade pierced her skin.

Once.

Twice.

Blood trickled down her side. Warm. Like honey. She kept her eyes on the nest. Then she heard a metallic click, followed by the sound of a man's voice.

"Drop your weapon," the man said.

Marshall didn't drop the knife. In one swift motion he turned toward the direction that the man's voice had come from and threw it overhand, with great force, the shiny steel blade and the black plastic handle whizzing through the air like a miniature airplane propeller, seeming—from Janelle's chemically-fueled, hyperaware perspective—to churn its way across the clearing in super slow motion, finally thudding definitively into something or someone about a hundred feet away.

Marshall lunged toward the SUV and grabbed the pistol from the driver seat, and then he ran to the other side of the vehicle and leaned over the front fender and the hood. Which kept most of his body shielded by the engine compartment. Which housed a ridiculously expensive state-of-the-art power plant that probably could have stopped a cannonball.

"Drop *your* weapon," he shouted, pointing the barrel of the pistol toward Janelle's face. "Drop it, or I'll blow her head off."

# 18

The knife had missed Wahlman's right shoulder by about two inches. He pulled it out of the decaying tree that he'd ducked behind, folded the blade into the handle and slid it into his pocket.

Wahlman owned a very nice handgun, but he wasn't allowed to carry it. Not yet. His application for a concealed weapons permit was still pending. Still swimming in a sea of red tape down in Frankfort. So the .40 caliber semi-automatic pistol he was holding didn't belong to him. It belonged to Lancaster, the security supervisor at River City Downs.

Wahlman tucked the gun into the back of his waistband. The man in the plaid flannel shirt had positioned himself behind the engine compartment of the white SUV, making the .40 cal of little use—at least for the moment. But Wahlman had something else with him, something that could possibly be of great use, something that could possibly enable him to circle around and approach the man in the plaid flannel shirt from the other side of the clearing,

72

something that could possibly take Janelle out of the deadly equation for a while by obstructing her from view.

Wahlman had borrowed the pistol from Lancaster.

And the grenade.

Smoke, or tear gas. He still wasn't sure. There were no markings on it, not even a warning statement.

Which was unusual. As a Master-At-Arms in the United States Navy, Wahlman had been trained and signed off on practically every canister-type grenade in existence. Invariably, the ones produced by legitimate contractors were clearly marked, sometimes in several different languages. Active and inactive ingredients, propellants, manufacturer, serial number, expiration date. Sometimes more than that. Sometimes a lot more. Sometimes there was more writing on a canister than there was blank space.

The fact that absolutely nothing had been stamped or etched onto this particular device was a good indication that this particular device had been purchased illegally. Which, as it turned out, was a very serious crime in the United States of America in 2101, subject to very serious fines and incarceration times. Smoke, or tear gas. It didn't matter to the Department of Homeland Security. The penalties were the same. But it mattered to Wahlman. He needed smoke. Tear gas might disable the man in the plaid flannel shirt for a while, but it would also disable Wahlman for a while. He didn't have a mask. A pressurized canister filled with a lachrymator agent would put him in the same eye-stinging, snot-gushing, throat-tightening boat as the man in the plaid flannel shirt. Which made the decision to use the grenade at all a pretty big gamble. Kind of like betting on a horse. Only you didn't get any points for second or third place. You either went home with the trophy or you went home dead.

Wahlman decided to give the man in the plaid flannel shirt one more chance to give himself up.

"The police are on the way," Wahlman said. "Drop your weapon and put your hands in the air and—"

"Did you hear me?" the man in the plaid flannel shirt said. "I'm going to blow her head off. I'll do it. Don't think I won't."

"Why did you kill Rokki Rhodes?"

"Shut up."

"Obsession can be a dangerous thing," Wahlman said. "It hardly ever ends well. Believe me."

"You're an idiot. Janelle was my girlfriend. We were going to be married."

"So it didn't work out. Now you're going to kill her? What kind of sense does that make?"

"We're going to be together forever," the man in the plaid flannel shirt said. "That's what kind of sense it makes."

It was starting to sound as though the man in the plaid flannel shirt was not only planning to kill Janelle, but himself as well. Which made him exponentially more dangerous. In Wahlman's experience, it was nearly impossible to reason with someone who had fallen into a hole that deep.

Even so, he tried to keep the conversation going.

"Keep talking," he said. "We can work this out."

"You want to know why I killed the stripper?" the man

in the plaid flannel shirt said. "Get your ass out here where I can see you. Then we'll talk."

Wahlman didn't get his ass out there where the man in the plaid flannel shirt could see him. Instead, he gripped the black market grenade he'd taken from Lancaster and pulled the pin and squeezed the lever and hoped for the best.

# 19

A billowing plume of smoke shot out. Which was good. It was exactly what Wahlman had wanted to happen. He launched the device in a high arc, hoping to land it on the other side of the white SUV where the man in the plaid flannel shirt was standing.

But the canister didn't land over there. In fact, it didn't land at all. Wahlman had thrown it too hard. He'd put too much muscle into it. The grenade had gotten stuck, somewhere up in the treetops.

Which was not good.

Now there was a nice thick purple cloud rolling out, but it was way up in the air and of absolutely no use to Wahlman.

Or so he thought.

But he was wrong about that. Because out of the nice thick purple cloud came a different kind of cloud, a swirling black funnel of anger, a buzzing squadron of black dots, descending as a single unit, with a single purpose, to eliminate the sudden threat, to attack the nearest and largest target, which just happened to be the man in the plaid flannel shirt.

He started shouting.

And screaming.

And dancing around.

He waved his arms frantically in an effort to bat the hornets away, but there must have been a thousand of them. They covered his body like too many sprinkles on a sundae.

Wahlman trotted across the clearing, toward the SUV. Janelle was on the ground, lying on her back. The hornets weren't paying any attention to her. Maybe because she was so low. And flat. And still. Wahlman picked her up and slid her into the driver seat, and then he climbed in and squeezed past her, and past the center console, and he plopped into the passenger seat and reached over and pulled the door shut.

"Are you all right?" he said.

"I think I'm bleeding," Janelle said.

Her speech was slurred, and her eyes weren't tracking right. It was possible that she'd taken a hit to the head, or that she'd been drugged. Or both. Wahlman looked her over. There was a bright red spot on the lower part of her shirt.

Wahlman lifted the hem.

"I need to get you to the hospital," he said.

"Marshall has the keys."

"The man in the plaid flannel shirt?"

"Yes."

Wahlman turned and looked out the passenger side window. Marshall was the one on the ground now, lying on

77

his back, staring up at the canopy. His face and hands were swollen. Fat and lumpy, as if someone had inflated them with a bicycle pump. He was having trouble breathing. Maybe an allergic reaction, Wahlman thought, but not necessarily. The venom from that many stings would probably put anyone down, allergic or not. Even a man as large and fit as Marshall.

The gun he'd been holding was gone. As were most of the hornets.

"Is there a first aid kit in the car?" Wahlman said.

"It's a rental," Janelle said. "I don't know."

Wahlman ripped his shirt open and started to take it off, intending to use it as a dressing.

"You've been stabbed," he said "I need to stop the bleeding."

"I have some tissues in my purse," Janelle said. "Maybe—"

Her voice trailed off. Wahlman grabbed the purse and opened it and found the tissues. He figured they would be better than his shirt. More absorbent, and less likely to cause an infection. He pulled the entire stack out of the little plastic package they were in and instructed Janelle to press them against the puncture wounds as hard as she could.

Janelle looked at the tissues.

And then she looked at Wahlman.

She seemed lost.

"Do you understand what I'm telling you?" Wahlman said.

"Can you say it again?"

Wahlman placed the tissues in her hand, and then he guided her hand to the wounds.

"Like this," he said.

Janelle nodded.

Wahlman climbed out of the car and walked over to where Marshall was lying. It appeared that Marshall wasn't having trouble breathing anymore. It appeared that he wasn't breathing at all.

Wahlman reached down to feel for a pulse, but before he had a chance to palpate the carotid artery on the left side of Marshall's neck, a pair of bloodshot eyes opened widely, and a pair of congested lungs gasped deeply, and a pair of red and bubbly hands reached up and grabbed him by the throat.

Suddenly, it was Wahlman who couldn't breathe. He tried to break the grip, tried to pry Marshall's thumbs away from his windpipe, but it was no use. It was like trying to loosen a rusty bolt with a popsicle stick. Just wasn't going to happen.

The pistol.

The .40 cal.

Wahlman reached around to the back of his waistband, but it wasn't there. It must have slipped out at some point, probably while he was scrambling through the interior of the SUV, trying to maneuver Janelle and himself away from the ill-tempered swarm of hornets. The gun was probably on the backseat floorboard, with a nice full magazine and one in the chamber and of absolutely no use to anyone at the moment.

Wahlman managed to suck in a little oxygen, but not nearly enough to meet his current demands. His heart was pounding like a jackhammer, and his arms and legs felt as though someone had tied anchors to them. The knife

Marshall had thrown was still in his back pocket. He could feel it. But it had slipped down into a horizontal position, and he couldn't get to it. The angle was wrong. He couldn't slide his fingers far enough down into the pocket.

Which meant that he was going to have to fight with his bare hands. Which ordinarily wouldn't have been a problem. But Marshall had extremely long arms. If he and Wahlman had been engaged in a boxing match, an observer might have noted that Marshall had the reach on Wahlman. A distinct advantage in a boxing match, or a cage fight, or a desperate struggle at the top of a park.

Marshall had extremely long arms, and they were locked at the elbows, and it was impossible for Wahlman to land a solid punch. He tried, again and again, but the blows just didn't have enough force behind them. They didn't knock Marshall out, and they didn't break his nose, and they didn't cause him to loosen his grip. If anything, his thumbs seemed to dig in deeper with every punch.

Wahlman tried not to panic. He tried to break the grip again, and couldn't again. He tried kneeing Marshall in the ribs, and he tried ripping the sweaty hair out of his head, and he tried pinching the blistered skin off of his face. Nothing was working. Nothing was going Wahlman's way, and his muscles were getting weaker by the second, and multicolored dots were dancing in front of his eyes, and he started thinking that maybe this was it, that he'd somehow allowed this lowlife piece of shit to get the better of him.

Or at least to break even. Because it didn't seem likely

that Marshall was going to make it either. Not without immediate medical attention.

So the race was on.

The race to see who died first.

# 20

Janelle knew where she was.

She knew that she was at the top of Iroquois Park. She'd been there many times as a teenager. Sometimes with a boyfriend, sometimes with a group, sometimes all by herself. She knew where she was, but she couldn't remember how she'd gotten there, and she couldn't imagine why those guys were fighting, out there in the clearing.

It appeared that they were trying to kill each other.

But why?

Janelle tried to think, tried to piece some things together, tried to assemble the jumble of images swirling through her brain. She'd been drunk plenty of times, but never like this. Something was wrong. She needed to call her dad. He would know what to do. He would come to the park, and soon everything would be all right. Soon everything would be back to normal.

Janelle reached into her purse and pulled out her cell phone.

No service.

Of course. You never could get a good signal up here. Because of the density of the forest. Janelle had known that for as long as she'd known anything. She just hadn't been thinking. She'd forgotten. Which wasn't like her.

Something was definitely wrong.

She needed to do something. She needed to get away from this crazy place.

She reached for the ignition.

No keys.

She grabbed her purse, turned it upside down, emptied the contents onto the passenger seat.

No keys.

They had to be somewhere, Janelle thought. She reached down and felt around on the floor. She felt behind the brake and the gas pedal, and she leaned over and checked the passenger side, and she twisted around and checked the back seat, and the floorboard back there, and she didn't see anything except an empty soda cup and an empty French fry box.

And a pistol.

She picked up the gun and looked at it and wondered how it had gotten there. Her father had taught her how to shoot when she was younger, but she'd never felt the need or the desire to purchase a gun for herself. Especially out in California, where the ownership and carry laws were much stricter.

She checked the magazine, and the chamber. The gun was fully loaded, and the safety had been switched off. Whoever had been carrying the weapon had been ready to use it. One squeeze of the trigger was all it would take.

Janelle looked out the window again. Her vision was starting to clear. One of the men looked familiar. Then they both looked familiar. Then it all came flooding back.

Marshall. He'd kidnapped her. He'd stabbed her with a knife.

The other guy, the one whose face was currently a disturbing shade of purple, had helped her. He'd picked her up and had carried her to the car.

She set the gun on the passenger seat and lifted the bottom of her shirt, looked down at her abdomen and carefully peeled back the stack of facial tissues. The bleeding had stopped, for the most part, although the wound closest to her belly button was still oozing a little.

The blade must not have penetrated very deeply, she thought. Half an inch, maybe. Just the tip. She would probably need stitches, and a course of antibiotics, but she didn't think that any internal organs had been damaged.

That being the case, she couldn't think of any reason why she shouldn't climb out of the SUV and try to help the man who'd helped her.

# 21

Wahlman struggled to maintain consciousness. He was teetering on the edge, knowing that the battle would be lost if something didn't happen soon.

Then something did happen.

The driver side door of the SUV swung open, and Janelle staggered out into the clearing and aimed the barrel of the pistol she was holding at Marshall's head.

"Let go of him," she said.

"Is this your boyfriend?" Marshall said.

"He's the good guy. You're the bad guy. Let go of him."

"I'll let go of him when he's dead."

Marshall's speech was garbled, barely comprehensible, as if he'd recently shoved a heaping spoonful of mashed potatoes into his mouth. Wahlman figured his tongue was swollen, from the hornet stings.

"Last chance," Janelle said. "Let go of him, and put your hands behind your head."

"Or what?"

"Or you're not going to have a head."

Marshall laughed.

"Is that a line from one of your movies?" he said. "Get real. You're not going to—"

Janelle pulled the trigger.

A bullet thudded into the dirt, inches from Marshall's right ear. An expression of sheer terror washed over his face. He loosened his grip. His arms fell to his sides.

Wahlman rolled away, coughing and gasping and greedily sucking in as much of the sweet and woodsy park air as he possibly could.

Janelle aimed the barrel of the pistol at the center of Marshall's chest.

"Hands behind your head," she shouted.

Marshall put his hands behind his head.

"Now what?" he said.

"Now we wait," Janelle said. "Gunshots attract attention. Remember? The cops should be here any minute."

Marshall took a ragged breath, and then another, and then he coughed and his eyes glazed over and his chest stopped rising and falling.

Wahlman advised Janelle to keep the gun on him anyway, unsure if Marshall was really dead this time and unwilling to crawl over there to find out.

Two LPD cruisers showed up, probably the same cars that had been parked nose-to-nose down at the main entrance. Wahlman figured that the sound of the gunshot had indeed attracted them, and that the smoke hovering above the treetops had led them to the right location.

A female officer climbed out of one of the cars, and a

male officer climbed out of the other, and they made it clear—immediately and in no uncertain terms—that Janelle was to drop the weapon she was holding, and that she was to lie face down on the ground with her fingers laced together behind her head. They ordered Wahlman to join her, and then they checked on Marshall, and they shook their heads somberly, and they made a compulsory effort to revive him, followed by a trip to one of the cruisers for a blanket to spread over his face.

The female officer cuffed Janelle and took her aside to interview her, and the male officer cuffed Wahlman and took him aside to interview him, and when everything had been sorted out, the female officer uncuffed Janelle, and the male officer uncuffed Wahlman, and the four of them waited for the ambulance and the team from the coroner's office to arrive.

# 22

Four days later, Janelle Pierce stopped by Wahlman's house on her way to the airport. Natalie had wanted to invite some of her friends from the dorm over for a meet and greet, and Kasey had wanted to invite her parents.

Wahlman had said no to both of them.

"That's not what this is about," he'd said. "She's been traumatized. I'm sure she doesn't want a bunch of people hanging around asking for autographs."

"Can we at least meet her?" Natalie had said.

"Briefly," Wahlman had said. "Then you'll need to leave us alone, so we can talk."

"This is so exciting! Janelle Pierce, right here at our house!"

Wahlman nodded. Now the porch would have another story, one that he knew for a fact to be true.

The limo eased over to the curb at a little past noon. The driver climbed out and opened Janelle's door for her. The cuts on her belly had been stitched up by a plastic surgeon, who'd assured her that the scarring would be minimal.

Wahlman could tell by the way she walked that she was sore. He met her out on the sidewalk and offered his arm for support as they made their way up to the stoop and into his office.

"This is my wife, Kasey," Wahlman said. "And this is our daughter, Natalie."

Janelle smiled.

"Pleased to meet both of you," she said.

"Pleased to meet you as well," Kasey said. "I'm a big fan."

"Me too," Natalie said.

"Thank you," Janelle said. "My agent sent me a new script yesterday. I'm going to read it on the flight. It'll be nice to get back to work."

Nobody said anything for a few seconds.

"Well, I know that you and Rock have a lot to talk about," Kasey said. "So, again, nice to meet you. Maybe we can all get together for dinner sometime."

"That would be nice," Janelle said.

Kasey and Natalie smiled and waved goodbye and exited the office. Alice had slinked out earlier. She was a little shy around new people.

Wahlman gestured toward the church pew.

"Have a seat," he said. "Can I get you some coffee? Anything?"

"No thanks," Janelle said.

She gripped the armrest and eased herself down onto the bench. Wahlman sat beside her, a couple of feet to her left.

"Have you heard back from the people at the track?" he said.

"Yes. It's all taken care of."

"Lancaster's not going to press charges?"

"He says he won't. And to be honest, it didn't really take much to convince him. All I had to do was mention the black market smoke grenade."

"I appreciate you going to bat for me," Wahlman said. "What a relief."

Janelle smiled.

"I always try to do whatever I can for people who save my life," she said. "And I have some more good news for you."

"Really?"

"I don't know if you were aware of this or not, but my father's a criminal defense attorney. He uses private investigators all the time. I gave him your number."

"I don't even know what to say. Thank you. I look forward to hearing from him."

"He's a good man," Janelle said. "I think the two of you will get along well."

"How are your parents coping with everything that happened?" Wahlman said. "Are they okay?"

"My dad never did like Marshall," Janelle said. "So of course I've been getting a lot of *I told you so* lectures from him. My mom was pretty rattled for a couple of days. Crying a lot, all that. But they'll be okay. Just worried about their little girl, like any parents would be. Which reminds me, I better get going. I have one more stop to make before I go to the airport."

Wahlman nodded. He knew where Janelle was going to

stop. She'd mentioned it earlier, on the phone.

Janelle knew that it wasn't her fault that Rokki Rhodes had been murdered, but she wanted to be as supportive as possible toward the grieving family anyway. Emotionally, and financially. Wahlman hadn't questioned her plans for a visit, but he wondered how Rokki's parents would react when they saw her walk through their door. Because of the remarkable resemblance. He wondered if they would lose it. Break down and start sobbing uncontrollably. He figured they would. He figured anybody would.

But he guessed he would never know for sure.

And he guessed it was better that way.

"I'll walk you to your car," he said.

"Tell Kasey and Natalie I said bye."

"I will. This was a big deal for them. Natalie wanted to invite some of her friends from college."

"Maybe next time."

"Sure."

"You think they would want to come outside with us?" Janelle said. "I could get my driver to take a picture of us all together."

"They would love that," Wahlman said.

And they did.

Thanks so much for reading RICOCHET!

For occasional updates and special offers, please sign up for my newsletter.

Love Jack Reacher? If so, I think you'll also love Nicholas Colt in AMERICAN P.I.

"This is a character I'm eager to follow through many adventures to come," says bestselling author Tess Gerritsen.

All of my books are lendable, so feel free to share them with a friend at no additional cost.

All reviews are much appreciated!

Thanks again, and happy reading!

Jude

Printed in the USA
CPSIA information can be obtained
at www.ICGtesting.com
LVHW050728230124
768661LV00011B/646